Tara
the Tuesday
Fairy

For Charlotte Tilley,
with lots of love and fairy magic

Special thanks to
Sue Mongredien

No part of this work may be reproduced, stored in a retrieval system,
or transmitted in any form or by any means, electronic, mechanical,
photocopying, recording, or otherwise, without written permission
of the publisher. For information regarding permission, write to
Rainbow Magic Limited c/o HIT Entertainment,
830 South Greenville Avenue, Allen, TX 75002-3320.

ISBN-10: 0-545-06756-1
ISBN-13: 978-0-545-06756-0

Previously published as *Talullah the Tuesday Fairy*
by Orchard U.K. in 2006.

All rights reserved. Published by Scholastic Inc., 557 Broadway,
New York, NY 10012, by arrangement with Rainbow Magic Limited.

SCHOLASTIC, LITTLE APPLE, and associated logos are
trademarks and/or registered trademarks of Scholastic Inc.
RAINBOW MAGIC is a trademark of Rainbow Magic Limited.
Reg. U.S. Patent & Trademark Office and other countries.

12 11 10 9 8 7 6 5 4   10 11 12 13/0

Printed in the U.S.A.

First Scholastic printing, August 2008

Tara
the Tuesday
Fairy

by Daisy Meadows

SCHOLASTIC INC.

New York   Toronto   London   Auckland   Sydney
Mexico City   New Delhi   Hong Kong   Buenos Aires

The
Fairyland
Palace.

Time
Tower

Windy
Lake

Tippingto
Towr

Morristown
Aquarium

The Tall
Toy
Store

Fashion
Fu

Fountain

Dancing
Days

Town
Hall

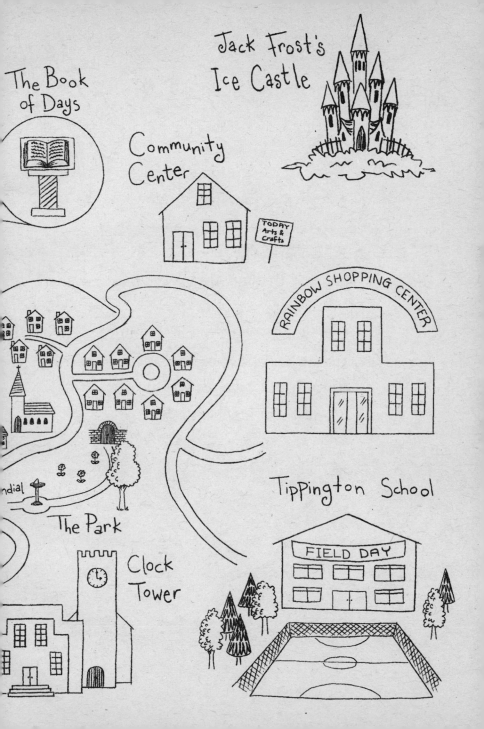

Icy wind now fiercely blow!
To the Time Tower I must go.
Goblins will all follow me
And steal the Fun Day Flags I need.

I know that there will be no fun,
For fairies or humans once the flags are gone.
Storm winds, take me where I say.
My plan for trouble starts today!

Contents

Field Day Sparkle

"Come on, Rachel! You can do it!"
Kirsty Tate cheered as she watched her
friend sprint down the sunny field. Today
was Tippington Schools' Field Day. The
three local schools had come together to
compete in all sorts of different games
and sports. Kirsty was staying with her
best friend, Rachel Walker, in

Tippington during school break, so she had come along to watch.

The 100-yard dash was the last race of the morning, and Rachel was doing really well. She was neck and neck with one other girl as they sprinted toward the finish line.

"Come on, Rachel, keep going!"
Kirsty yelled. The two runners were so
close, it was impossible to guess who was
going to win. Then, at the very last
moment, Rachel surged past the other
girl with a final burst of speed, and
crossed the finish line.

"Yay! Rachel wins!"
Kirsty cheered,
jumping up and down.
She beamed at some
of the other children
who had watched the
race, but they all
looked unhappy.
*They must have wanted
the other girl to win
really badly,* Kirsty
thought.

Rachel came over a few moments later, smiling. Her face was flushed. "Phew — that was a close one," she panted.

"You were amazing!" Kirsty smiled. "What an exciting race!"

"Well, I thought so," Rachel said. "But have you noticed that everyone else seems really bored?"

Kirsty looked around. It was true. A girl nearby was scuffing the grass with her foot and complaining to her dad that she was too cold. One of the older boys was saying that he was

hungry. Even some of the
teachers seemed bored.

A startling thought
struck both girls at
exactly the same time.
"It must be because the
Tuesday Fun Flag is missing,"
Kirsty said in a low voice.

"That's what I was about to say,"
Rachel agreed. "That explains why
nobody is having fun today!"

Rachel and Kirsty shared an exciting
secret: they were on a mission to help the
fairies! Jack Frost had stolen the seven
Fun Day Flags. The Fun Day Fairies
used them to bring fun to everyone in
Fairyland and in the human world. But
once the flags were in Jack Frost's ice

castle, his goblins started having too much fun. They played lots of tricks on Jack Frost!

Fed up with the goblins, Jack Frost sent a breeze to blow the flags into the human world. Little did he know that his goblins missed their fun and games so much they had snuck away to find the flags again.

"We'll have to look out for Tara the Tuesday Fairy," Rachel said, glancing around hopefully. "The sooner we can find the Tuesday Fun Flag, the better for everyone!"

Just then, an announcement came over the speakers. "This morning's races are now finished. Please make your way to the gym, where the

prizes will be presented before lunch.
Thank you."

The Field Day was taking place at
Rachel's school, so she led Kirsty inside
to the gym. A stage had been set up
along one wall for the first, second, and

third prize winners to receive their medals.

"I'll meet you afterward, OK?" Rachel said, joining the group of winners waiting to collect their prizes.

"OK," Kirsty agreed, going to sit at the back of the gym to watch. As she took her seat, she noticed that a table set up behind her had a big, impressive golden cup on it. *That must be the trophy for the school that wins the most events*, she guessed.

A woman in a plum-colored suit came and stood on the stage. "Good morning,"

she said, "I'm Jennie Bailey, Tippington's principal, and I'm so happy to be here to award the medals today."

As the principal went on speaking, Kirsty heard a tiny sound and turned around. To her surprise, the golden trophy was glittering more brightly than ever. Nobody else had noticed, because everyone was sitting with their backs to the trophy table. Then the trophy lid rattled, and a stream of turquoise sparkles came drifting out from inside the cup!

Rhyming Clue

Kirsty recognized fairy magic when she saw it! But how could she go over and investigate without everyone noticing and wondering what she was doing? Luckily, at that moment, everybody else in the audience started clapping loudly for the children who had won prizes.

Kirsty quietly slipped out of her seat

and tiptoed over to the trophy. Very
carefully, she reached out, lifted the lid,
and peeked inside. There, zooming
around inside the cup, was a tiny fairy!

Kirsty and Rachel had met all the Fun
Day Fairies the day before, and Kirsty
recognized Tara the Tuesday Fairy right
away. "Hello, Tara!" she whispered,
smiling.

Tara beamed thankfully as she saw
Kirsty's face, and quickly fluttered out of
the trophy. She had long, brown, curly
hair, which was swept up into a high
ponytail. She wore a cropped blue
jacket and blue pants, and had a
pretty flower necklace around
her neck.

"Thanks for letting
me out," she replied in
a whisper. "I came
here to find the
Tuesday Fun Flag, but
I didn't mean to get
stuck in that trophy!"

"Well you showed
up at just the right time,"
Kirsty whispered back. "Nobody is
having fun here."

Tara opened her mouth to reply, but then got distracted by what the principal was saying.

"I'm sorry to announce," the principal said, "that the medals and certificates for our winners have been misplaced. The winners will receive tokens instead for now, and we will break for lunch. I'm sure we will find the real prizes soon."

There were a few mumbles of disappointment, and then the audience started leaving the gym. Tara promptly dove into Kirsty's pocket and out of sight.

"I was looking forward to my prize,"

Kirsty heard one little girl saying sadly.
"This Field Day is no fun at all."

Rachel came over to Kirsty and Tara,
looking upset. But
she brightened up
when she saw the
little fairy peeking
out of Kirsty's
pocket. "Oh,
Tara, thank
goodness you're
here!" she said.
"Let's all go and
find a quiet spot to talk. We really need
to track down your flag."

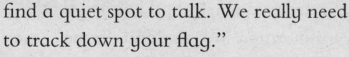

The three of them left the gym, and
Rachel led them to an empty hallway.
"Everyone is getting lunch, so we won't
be bothered here," she said.

"Tara, do you have any clues from the Book of Days?" Kirsty asked.

Rachel and Kirsty had learned that every morning in Fairyland, Francis, the Royal Time Guard, consulted a large book to check which day it was. Then he raised that day's flag up the flagpole. The day before, with all the Fun Day

Flags missing, a riddle had appeared
in the Book of Days instead. It had
helped the girls find Megan the Monday
Fairy's flag.

"Francis looked in the book this
morning. There was a new poem in it,"
Tara said. "It goes like this:

In the air, not on the ground
At Field Day, flags are all around.
Check the colored decorations
For Tuesday Fun Flag celebrations!"

"*Check the colored decorations. . . .*" Rachel repeated thoughtfully.

"That's right," Tara said. "The Tuesday Fun Flag is turquoise and sparkly, so —"

But before she could say another word, a closet door behind the girls suddenly burst open! Kirsty and Rachel jumped out of the way as a tangle of mops and brooms crashed to the ground. Out hopped two grinning goblins who had been listening to every word they said!

"Thanks for telling us the riddle," one of them cackled.

"Yes, now we know where to look for the flag," the other one added. "And we'll be taking it home with us!" With that, the goblins ran away down the hallway, chuckling gleefully.

Goblins Have a Head Start

"Oh, no!" Kirsty cried. "Where are they going?"

"Don't worry," Rachel said. "It's OK. I think I figured out the riddle. The clue is in the first line."

Tara looked around hurriedly. "Don't say another word," she warned, "in case there are any other sneaky goblins

nearby. Just take us to where you think
the flag might be."

"OK," Rachel said. "This way!"

Tara quickly waved her wand so that
all the mops and brooms jumped back
into the closet. The door
swung shut in a burst of
turquoise glitter.
Then Rachel led
Kirsty and Tara
back toward the
sports field.
Luckily, it was
empty now,
because everybody had gone to get
lunch. Tara could fly in the open air
without anyone seeing her. Kirsty pulled
a couple of apples from her bag, and the
girls ate them as they walked.

When they reached the field, Rachel pointed up at the strings of colored flags that fluttered in the breeze.

"The clue said the flag would be in the air, not on the ground, didn't it?" she said, pointing at the flags. "So I think it must be somewhere up there!"

"Great!" said Tara, clapping her hands in delight. Then she looked around with a determined gleam in her eye. "There are lots of turquoise flags, though, and I can't tell which is mine from here. We'll have to look at each of them closely to find the Tuesday flag."

Kirsty gazed down the length of the sports field. The flags were strung between poles in a large rectangular shape on the grass. They marked where the races were held. The girls and Tara were standing near the starting line at one corner of the rectangle. Strings of

flags stretched away from them in two
different directions. "I'll start looking
along this side," Kirsty said,
pointing to the line of flags
on her right.

"And I'll check the
flags above the starting
line," Rachel said,
turning to her left.

"Then I'll fly across
to the other side of the
field and look at the ones
above the finish line," Tara said,
fluttering away quickly.

Kirsty began walking along, checking
all the turquoise flags on her side. There
were hundreds of triangular flags in
white, red, orange, yellow, and
turquoise, flapping in the breeze. As she

walked, she looked carefully at all the
turquoise flags, hoping to see a telltale
sparkle or two of fairy magic. There was
no sign of the Tuesday Fun Flag!

Kirsty glanced down the line to see
how far she had to go. At that moment,
she spotted the sunlight glinting off of a
twinkly-looking turquoise flag at the
other end of the string. It was so sparkly
and bright, she was sure it must be the
Tuesday Fun Flag!

"Over here!" she called to Rachel and Tara, pointing at the flag. Then she looked back at the string of flags and her smile vanished. Two goblins had darted out from behind a tree, and they had seen where she was pointing!

"Oh no!" Kirsty cried, breaking into a run. But the goblins were much closer to the flag, and before Kirsty could get to it, they'd reached it with a cheer.

"Don't worry, they're not tall enough to get it down," Rachel called as she ran over. The goblins were too short to grab the flag, even if they stood on their tiptoes.

"That's what you think!" one of the goblins sneered. He crouched down with his hands together, making a step for the other goblin. The second goblin put his

foot on the "step," and his friend boosted him up into the air. As he flew upward, the goblin reached out and grabbed the flag firmly in his gnarled green fingers. He stuck out his tongue at the girls.

"What were you saying about us not being able to reach it?" he taunted gleefully. "Well, we just did. Now this flag means lots of Tuesday fun for us goblins!"

Girls Get Crafty

The goblin tugged at the flag with a grin on his face, but then his grin vanished. The flag wouldn't budge!

Kirsty held her breath, hoping that the flag was stuck to the string and that the goblin wouldn't be able to pull it free. But then, the triangular turquoise flag

suddenly came loose. As it did, it
unfolded to its usual rectangular shape in
the goblin's hand. Kirsty could see the
distinctive sun pattern marked out on it
in turquoise glitter.

"Got it!" the goblin roared in triumph,
as he dropped to the ground.

"Run!" shouted the other goblin, sprinting across the field away from the girls and Tara.

"After them!" called Rachel, racing off.

Kirsty was close behind. "Come back with that flag!" she yelled.

But the goblins didn't stop. They ran the length of the field and then dove into a tent that had been set up in case of rain.

The girls and Tara followed them inside and looked around.

There were mats stacked
up for the high jump,
sacks for the sack race,
hula hoops, hurdles,
cones, and all sorts of
other equipment
needed for Field
Day, but there
was no sign of
any green
goblins.

"There are
lots of good
hiding places in
here," Rachel
muttered to her
friends. "We'd better
start searching for
those goblins!"

Kirsty checked around the piles of mats, but the goblins weren't hiding behind them. Rachel looked behind the rack of hula hoops, but there were no goblins there, either. Tara waved her wand over a large crate of tennis balls, and with a stream of turquoise sparkles, all of the balls bounced out in a neat formation. "No

goblins in there," she said, fluttering over
the empty crate and waving her wand a
second time.

Instantly, the tennis
balls bounced back
into the crate,
lining
themselves
up neatly.
Then,
Rachel went
over to a pile of
sacks. As she
drew closer, she saw that there were two
sacks that were upside down. Poking out
of the bottom of each one was a pair of
big, green goblin feet! Then she noticed
that a corner of the twinkly turquoise

flag was poking out of one sack, too!
The goblins had put empty sacks over
their heads, trying to hide.

Without a word, Rachel waved Kirsty
and Tara over and pointed at the sacks.

Then she pulled her friends behind a
stack of hurdles so that they could
whisper together.

"We have to think up a really good way to get the goblins out of there," Rachel said.

"Yes — and a way to get the flag back, too!" Kirsty agreed in a low voice. She glanced around the tent.

"Maybe we could tickle the goblin holding the flag until he lets go," Rachel

suggested in a whisper. "You know how much goblins hate being tickled."

Tara looked doubtful. "Yes, but the flag is already in the sack with the goblin," she pointed out. "He might just pull it further inside to keep it safe."

Rachel and Tara looked at Kirsty hopefully. Rachel could see that her friend was thinking hard. After a few moments, she said, "I think I've got an idea." She grinned at Rachel and Tara. "And it just might work!"

Three-Legged Fun

"The goblins are standing right next to
each other, so let's give them their very
own three-legged race," Kirsty giggled,
pulling a jump rope out of a crate.
"Tara, could you use your magic to tie
this rope to one goblin's right leg and the
other goblin's left leg?" she whispered
with a grin.

Rachel clapped a hand over her mouth
to stop herself from laughing out loud at
the idea. Tara was smiling, too, as she
waved her wand in the air. A moment
later, the jump rope flew obediently over
to the goblins. In a turquoise blur of fairy
sparkles, it wound itself
around the left leg of
the first goblin and
the right leg of the
second goblin, before
tying itself tightly in
a knot. The rope
paused and then
added a loopy
bow, with a
final burst
of bright
sparkles.

Tara chuckled softly. "They won't be able to run very far with my flag now," she said, her eyes twinkling.

"Now I'll grab the flag!" whispered Rachel.

She tiptoed over to the sack with the Fun Day Flag sticking out of it. Very quietly, she reached out, grasped the shimmering turquoise fabric, and yanked it sharply. She must have caught the goblin by surprise, because the flag immediately came free.

"Hey!" the goblin yelled. "Who did that? Who grabbed the flag? Was it you?"

"Me? No!" the other goblin replied. "It must be those pesky girls. Quick, we've got to get out of these sacks!"

Rachel ran back to the others as the two goblins threw their sacks off and tried to chase after the girls, not realizing that their legs were tied together.

"Whoa!" the first one yelled as he was pulled over by the second. "What happened?"

The second goblin tried to get back on his feet, but he couldn't stand up. Then he noticed the jump rope around his leg. "They played a trick on us!" he moaned. "We're tied together!" His fingers pulled at the knot, but it wouldn't come undone. It was fastened tightly with fairy magic!

After a moment, he gave up. The two goblins tried to stand up together and walk. Rachel and Kirsty couldn't resist watching as the goblins swayed, wobbled, and then fell over again. It was so funny!

"Hey — stop pushing me!" the first goblin screeched.

"You're pushing *me*!" the second goblin snapped. "And now those girls have our flag!"

"Sorry," Tara said flying out in front of the goblins. "But it's my flag, and if you two try to steal it again, I'll tell Jack Frost you were trying to sneak it back into his ice castle!" She grinned. "Don't worry, though. As soon as my flag is back in Fairyland where it belongs, that rope will magically undo itself."

The goblins' shoulders slumped at her words. They knew they were beaten. They sighed and stumbled off, still grumbling about being tied together with the jump rope.

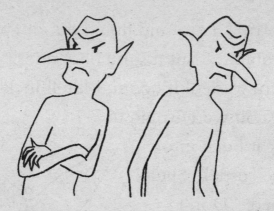

"Here you are, Tara," Rachel said, handing the sparkly flag to the little fairy.

"Thank you," Tara said happily, as she waved her wand to shrink the flag to its Fairyland size. In order to fit into the human world, the flag had magically grown bigger. "Now I'd better zoom back to Fairyland, to recharge my wand with Tuesday magic."

The girls knew that the Fun Day magic needed to be collected by the Fun Day Fairies in a special way. Tara would have to return to Fairyland and give the Tuesday Fun Flag to Francis, who would run it to the top of the flagpole on the

Time Tower. Then Tara would
stand in the courtyard below and
hold up her wand. When the sun's rays
struck the glittery pattern on the Fun
Day Flag, a stream of Tuesday magic

would be reflected from the flag down to Tara's wand.

"I won't be long," Tara said. "And when I get back, I'll be able to make this Field Day full of fun!"

Tuesday Fun for Everyone!

"Great," Rachel said happily. "See you soon!"

They waved good-bye to the smiling fairy as she disappeared in a flurry of bright fairy dust. And then, seconds later, a teacher walked into the tent, looking surprised to see the girls standing there.

"Hello," the teacher said with a puzzled look on her face. Then she smiled. "Oh, are you here to help me get the sacks for the sack race?"

"Um . . . yes," Rachel said quickly, relieved that there weren't still two sneaky goblins in the sacks!

"Great," the teacher replied, picking up a stack of the sacks. "If you could each take another pile of these, that would be really helpful. The afternoon events are about to start in a few minutes."

"No problem," Kirsty said politely, picking up a pile of sacks.

"I hope Tara comes back soon," Rachel whispered to Kirsty, as they left the tent. "Look at everyone's faces!"

Kirsty looked around as she and

Rachel carried their sacks across the field and set them down by the starting line. She could see that lots of children were drifting back to the field after lunch, but they all still looked miserable.

At that moment, an announcement came over the speakers. "The sack race is

about to begin. Would all competitors
please come to the starting line to take
their places?"

While the morning's events had only
been for the students of the three schools,
the afternoon's activities were fun races
and games anyone could enter, including
guests, parents, and teachers. Kirsty and
Rachel were looking forward to racing
together in lots of events, including the
sack race.

They watched as a crowd of boys and
girls came to the starting line, all looking
gloomy about the race.

"My sack feels really scratchy," one girl
grumbled as she stepped into it.

"I wish I hadn't entered this race," her
friend muttered.

Kirsty and Rachel stepped into their

own sacks, looking around for any sign of Tara. "I hope everything's all right," Kirsty whispered to Rachel. "What if something happened to Tara and her flag?"

"On your mark . . . get set . . ." a teacher called, holding up a whistle. "GO!" As she blew the whistle,

turquoise glitter showered all over the
sack racers! The teacher looked surprised,
but Kirsty and Rachel grinned at one
another.

"Fairy dust!" Kirsty giggled.

"Tara must be back with her Fun Day
magic!" Rachel said happily. "She's just
in time!"

"Oops — the race has started!" Kirsty laughed, suddenly remembering that they were supposed to be bouncing along in their sacks. "Come on, Rachel!"

There were squeals of laughter from the other children, and breathless shouts as they all jumped along in their sacks, trying to reach the finish line first.

"This is so much fun!" Rachel

heard one boy shout,
with a big grin on his face.
"Can't catch me!" a girl
yelled, between bursts
of giggles.
Kirsty and Rachel
couldn't help
laughing, too. "Fairy
magic is amazing!"
Kirsty said as
they jumped
along together.
"Suddenly,
everyone is having
fun again!"
"And it's all thanks
to Tara," Rachel
laughed. "Hooray for Fun Day magic!"

A big cheer came from the crowd when a little girl won the race.

Rachel and Kirsty were the last two to hop over the finish line, but they were so happy, they didn't mind.

Then a special announcement came over the speakers. "We have some good news: the medals and prize certificates have just been found," came a cheerful

voice. "Everyone will be able to collect them before they go home!"

"Hooray!" cheered all the children.

"It looks like the rest of Field Day is going to be full of fun now," Kirsty said happily.

"I think so, too," came a silvery voice from just behind her ear.

Kirsty and Rachel smiled at the little fairy who had reappeared beside them.

"Thanks, Tara," Rachel said. "Everyone's having such a good time now."

"Well, I came to thank you for helping

me," Tara replied. "Now I can spread
my Tuesday magic everywhere. Before
I go, I just wanted to wish you luck in
the next race. Have you heard what
it is?"

"No," Kirsty replied. "What?"

Tara smiled mysteriously. "I think
you'll like it." She laughed. "Good-bye
for now!" She waved her wand and a

swirl of turquoise sparkles tumbled all around her. Then she was gone.

Before Kirsty or Rachel could say another word, another announcement began. "The next race will be the three-legged race. All competitors, please line up at the starting line to have your legs tied."

Rachel and Kirsty burst out laughing. "We're definitely going to enter this one," Rachel said, grabbing Kirsty's hand.

Kirsty nodded. "We couldn't be any worse than the goblins!"

THE FUN DAY FAIRIES

Megan and Tara have their flags back.
Now Rachel and Kirsty must help

Willow
the Wednesday
Fairy!

Arts and Crafts

"This is great." Rachel Walker said, beaming at her best friend, Kirsty Tate, as they wandered around the Tippington Community Center Arts and Crafts Fair. "I don't know what to do first!"

The fair was in full swing. Wooden tables covered with long white cloths were arranged in a huge square, and each table

had been set up for different crafts. Rachel and Kirsty could see neat piles of velvet, satin, and silk fabrics for making patchwork quilts on one table, and knitting needles and baskets of fluffy wool on another. In one corner of the square, a man was demonstrating origami, and in another Rachel's mom, Mrs. Walker, was teaching scrapbooking. Each table had space for people to try the crafts themselves, and there were already long lines at some of them.

"This is great, isn't it?" Kirsty said, looking around. "And I just thought of something. With so much colorful fabric and paper around, this would be the perfect place to find one of the fairies' Fun Day Flags!"

Come flutter by Butterfly Meadow!

Butterfly Meadow #1: Dazzle's First Day
Dazzle is a new butterfly, fresh out of her cocoon. She doesn't know how to fly, and she's all alone! But Butterfly Meadow could be just what Dazzle is looking for.

Butterfly Meadow #2: Twinkle Dives In
Twinkle is feisty, fun, and always up for an adventure. But the nearby pond holds much more excitement than she expected!

■SCHOLASTIC
www.scholastic.com

A fairy for every day!

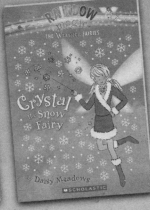

The Rainbow Fairies
Books #1-7

The Weather Fairies
Books #1-7

The Jewel Fairies
Books #1-7

The Pet Fairies
Books #1-7

The Fun Day Fairies
Books #1-7

SCHOLASTIC

www.rainbowmagiconline.com
www.scholastic.com

HIT entertainment

FAIRY